JUST THE MOON

by Dawn McMillan
illustrated by Priscilla Nielsen

Harcourt
SCHOOL PUBLISHERS

Printed in China

ISBN 10: 0-15-350445-5
ISBN 13: 978-0-15-350445-7

Ordering Options
ISBN 10: 0-15-350332-7 (Grade 2 Below-Level Collection)
ISBN 13: 978-0-15-350332-0 (Grade 2 Below-Level Collection)
ISBN 10: 0-15-357454-2 (package of 5)
ISBN 13: 978-0-15-357454-2 (package of 5)

4 5 6 7 8 9 10   0940   15 14 13 12 11 10 09

Lee and his father lived on a
houseboat. It floated in the river.

One night, Lee listened to the water washing against the side of the boat. The boat creaked and grunted as it moved with the water.

Suddenly, Lee felt smothered by the darkness around him. He found his father and sat down gently beside him.

"Father," he whispered. "I am afraid of the dark. I wish I had a lantern."

"You have no need to be afraid of the dark," replied Lee's father. You can see many beautiful things in the night. Look out there, over the water."

Lee could see fireflies dancing in the night air. "The fireflies are beautiful," Lee whispered. "A firefly is too small to be my lantern."

Lee looked up and saw the stars.
"The stars are beautiful, too," he
whispered. "A star is too far away
to be my lantern!"

"What about the moon?" asked Lee's father.

Lee stared at the round and yellow moon. Its light shone across the river. "Tonight the moon is a magnificent lantern," Lee laughed. "That is not always so. Some nights it is covered by clouds."

"Come, Lee," said his father. "Let us go to the market to buy you a lantern."

They stepped onto the dock and walked to the market.

The market was full of fragrant flowers and fruit. There were many different lanterns, too.

Lee found a lantern that was round and yellow. It was like the moon. "May I have this one, Father?" he pleaded.

"Of course, my son," said his father. "What a magnificent lantern."

Lee and his father returned to the houseboat. "Look, Father!" Lee cried. "My lantern shines across the water. It is just like the moon."

"Yes, but the clouds can't cover it up," said his father.

"Oh, look now! The moths like it, too! There *are* beautiful things to *see* in the night," Lee said excitedly.

"Oh, thank you, Father," said Lee.
"This is a magnificent lantern."

Think Critically

1. Why did Lee and his father go to the market?

2. Why did Lee say the moon couldn't always be his lantern?

3. What words would you use to tell about Lee's father?

4. What was the setting at the beginning of the story? How did it change during the story?

5. How do you feel when you're in the dark?

 **Social Studies**

Write a Paragraph Write a paragraph about the differences between shopping at a market and shopping at a store.

School-Home Connection Tell a family member about Lee and his father. Then talk about how a family member helped you feel better about a problem.

Word Count: 330